HEIDI
JOHANNA SPYRI
ADAPTED BY ROSEMARY HARRIS
ILLUSTRATED BY TOMI UNGERER

This edition first published 1983
by Ernest Benn Ltd. Sovereign Way,
Tonbridge, Kent TN9 1RW

First published in two volumes
by Diogenes Verlag under the titles
Heidis Lehr- und Wanderjahre and
Heidi Kann Brauchen, Was Es Gelernt Hat.

ISBN 0 510 00157-2
Printed and bound in Italy for Imago Publishing Ltd.

Ernest Benn

The little Swiss village of Dörfli lies high above an alpine valley, yet still a long way below the steep flower-scattered pastures, rocky slopes and rugged snow-capped mountains. A single footpath winds upwards to the heights from Dörfli; and one hot June morning a strong young woman was climbing it, towing by the hand a reluctant small girl muffled in heavy clothes topped by a big red scarf. The child's heat-glazed cheeks were red as apples, her shape as round, her feet in nailed boots barely able to carry her along. Suddenly she pulled her hand away, and plumped down heavily upon the path.

"Tired, Heidi?" asked her cousin Dettie.

"No — but I'm *hot*."

"Your Grandfather's home is only an hour's climb ahead of us now — Come along." Dettie was eager to move on, for she'd been well scolded by her friends in Dörfli for what she planned to do: take Heidi to live alone with her grim old grandfather. Even now one of these women came toiling after them, panting, "Wait for me, Dettie, I'm coming halfway, to the goatherd's hut. I've business with his mother — and I must talk to you. Listen: our old dragon of an 'Alp-Uncle' is no guardian for Heidi, and you know it! He's offended everybody with his hermit ways and surly tongue — and he never comes to church; not him!"

Dettie just looked stubborn, so her friend Barbie continued, "He was wild enough as a young man, God knows, and there were plenty of rumours about him later, too, when he was a soldier! People said his only son's death was a judgment on him for his godlessness —".

While the two women argued, Heidi had been free to look around her. Farther down the slope she spied a fascinating sight: young Peter, who looked after the villagers' goats in summer, was wandering the mountainside with his grazing herd. Now Dettie's eyes were off her Heidi ran to join him and climb beside him. Soon she was envying him his thin clothes and bare feet, and suddenly she sat down again, to struggle out of everything except her little shift. Peter grinned broadly, but said nothing — not even when she left all her clothes and heavy boots lying behind her in a heap. She jigged after him, enjoying her freedom and asking eager questions about the goats.

Dettie only missed Heidi when Barbie left her for the goatherd's hut. She called and looked about her anxiously. At last she saw Heidi some way below her climbing between rock and scrub with her new friend.

"Heidi," she called. "What are you thinking of, and where are your clothes?"

When Heidi rejoined her, with Peter, and pointed to the brilliant scarlet scarf marking the bundle far below, Dettie began to scold her furiously, and told Peter in her sharpest manner to run and fetch them. Afterwards they all climbed the last part of the way in company, so that Peter and his goats, Dettie and Heidi reached the plateau before 'Alp-Uncle's' hut together. They found the solitary grey-bearded old man sitting on an outside bench, smoking his pipe. He looked at them beneath his heavy eyebrows without a word of welcome; a stern and imposing figure, yet Heidi went to him straight away, saying, "Good evening, Grandfather," and held out her small hand. He took it briefly in his, but spoke to Peter.

"What are you hanging about here for? Take my goats, and off with you to the high pastures." Then, as Peter hurriedly obeyed, he turned back to Dettie. "Well, what's all this about?" he asked her harshly, with a piercing look.

"Good day, Uncle — you surely remember your own grandchild? I've brought Heidi here to live with you. I've had her

all these years since she was orphaned, but now I'm offered a fine new job where I can't take her with me.''

''Indeed!'' The old man gave her a dragon glare. ''And when she howls for you, what then?''

''Why, do as you like! You can't have a worse conscience than you have already,'' retorted Dettie.

Her uncle stood up, and glowered down at her more fiercely than before. ''Never let me see *you* here again,'' he said.

''Why, goodbye then, Uncle,'' said Dettie calmly. ''And you too, Heidi.'' She wasn't waiting for any more, but turned her back on them and began making her way as quickly as possible down the steep mountain path.

Left alone with Heidi, her grandfather settled himself in grim silence on the bench, indignantly puffing out clouds of smoke. Heidi herself promptly started on a voyage of discovery. Behind the hut were three ancient firtrees whose thick branches sighed together in the wind. Heidi listened, entranced. After a while she returned to Grandfather, unabashed, her dark eyes glowing with excitement. ''Can I see what you keep inside the hut?''

He stood up and led the way indoors. ''Bring your belongings with you,'' he commanded her.

''I don't need silly clothes,'' said Heidi, with some spirit.

Well, at least she's sensible, thought Grandfather. ''Put them away then, Heidi, in my cupboard.''

The hut was really one large room, simply furnished, with Grandfather's sleeping place opposite his hearth and cooking pot. The big cupboard held shirts and socks, plates, cups and glasses, smoked meat, cheese and bread; all his daily needs. Heidi pushed her bundle deep inside.

''Where shall I sleep, Grandfather?''

''Wherever you choose,'' he said shortly.

Heidi clambered up a short ladder into the loft, and looked around her at the sweet-smelling hay and small round open window. Everything about this new life immediately thrilled and attracted her. And she wasn't at all in awe of Grandfather's rough ways; after all, he didn't seem unkind, and so far he was a pleasant change from the tiresome, grumbling old woman who had chivvied her continually and kept her indoors while Dettie was out at work.

"It's beautiful up here, Grandfather!" she called out. "Come and see how beautiful." While she began making herself a comfortable hay bed, he discovered a heavy linen sack for her to use as coverlet.

"Well, now, what about a meal?" he suggested.

So they prepared it together. Grandfather toasted bread and goats' cheese, and set a mug of milk upon the table which Heidi helped to lay. After they'd eaten, she sat and watched him carpenter a three-legged stool. 'Alp-Uncle' was a splendid craftsman, and soon had it ready for her. The time passed very quickly, with one new interest following another — until the best one of all: Peter brought Grandfather's own two goats back from pasture. After they had been seen securely into their stalls at the back of the hut Heidi had fresh milk and bread for supper, then fell happily asleep in her nest of hay.

During the night the wind rose violently, shaking the firtrees and the hut. "The child — she'll be afraid," Grandfather muttered, mounting the ladder to the loft. The bright moonshine shone on Heidi's sleeping face, her whole expression was full of joy. After watching her a little while he returned to bed.

Next day Heidi woke to brilliant sunlight. Immediately she thought of Grandfather's goats — Little Swan and Little Bear — put on her simple dress and ran barefoot outside, where young Peter was already waiting with his herd.

"Clean yourself up a little, Heidi," said Grandfather, placing a tub of water for her in the sun. While she washed he told Peter: "Come, General of Goats, show me your haversack —" and he put in extra bread and cheese, together with a bowl for Heidi. "Now off with you both, to the high pastures."

Sunlight shimmered on the green slopes with all their flowers. Heidi was enchanted — she ran to and fro, picking blue gentians and yellow rockroses, thinking they would make her loft look and smell just like the alp.

"Heidi, Heidi! Old Uncle told you not to go too near the heights," called Peter. His herd was grazing where scrub gave place to barren stone, and here he flung himself down on the warm earth; Heidi sat mouse-still beside him, gazing round her. Never in her short life had she found anything so fine. She snuffed up sweet flowery scents and wished to stay there for ever . . .

"Peter! Wake up — see that big bird fly? Now where's it gone?"

"Eagle's nest," said Peter briefly.

"Shall we climb and find it?"

"Goats can't climb so high! Anyway, Uncle said you weren't to go rock-climbing." He began calling his herd around him, and Heidi watched Little Swan milked into her bowl, before she and Peter ate their midday meal. She had more bread and cheese than he did, and she gave him most of hers.

"Tell me the goats' names, Peter?"

Among them was big Turk, a natural bully; gentle Snowflake, and naughty little Greenfinch — so active that he

nearly fell down the ravine. Peter would have beaten him, but Heidi spoke so fiercely (and promised Peter more midday cheese) that the hungry goatherd swore never to beat his goats again.

They stayed till nearly sunset, when a rosy glow spread over the mountain tops and rich golden light upon the pastures.

"Is it always like this up here?" Heidi asked. She went home contentedly when Peter answered, "Yes".

Grandfather was waiting for them by the firtrees. She ran to tell him all about her day: ". . . but my flowers died, I won't pick them any more — they wanted to stay up there in sunshine. Grandfather, why does the eagle cry so harshly?"

"He's telling folk down in Dörfli they should live wild and free as he does, and stop telling tales about each other."

When Heidi asked him about the strange fiery light he told her: "That's the sun's way of telling the mountains he'll return tomorrow."

All summer long Peter and Heidi climbed to the high pastures. She grew brown and healthy living like a wild bird, but when the strong autumn winds blew Grandfather forbade her wanderings. "A little one like you could be blown away into the valley." Both Peter and the goats missed her badly — and Peter missed the extra cheese; but Heidi herself was happy with her Grandfather, watching him at carpentry, or making round goats'-cheeses. She loved to hear the rustling of the three old firs as the wind shook their branches till it seemed they danced above her head, as she herself danced underneath them.

The cold grew bitter, and the winds blew through Heidi's thickest clothing. When the snow came Peter stayed home with his mother and grandmother, the goats stayed in their stalls, and Heidi looked out on a world of whirling snowflakes falling so softly yet building so high that the hut windows wouldn't open, and Grandfather had to take his spade to dig a pathway. While he and Heidi were sitting cosily together by the fire someone banged loudly on the door, and in tumbled a snow-covered Peter, braving the icy afternoon to visit Heidi. He grinned at her delightedly.

"So, General, you've lost your summer army, and now it's winter school for you," said Grandfather.

Peter looked very downcast — he was no scholar, and it was more to his taste when the old man, smiling, began preparing supper. Since Heidi's coming Grandfather had made another bench, and the three of them could sit comfortably together at the table. When Peter had to leave at last he told them: "I'll come again. And Grandmother wants Heidi to visit her."

Grandfather wasn't pleased. Day after day he declared, "Not through this snow." But he gave way when the snow froze solid, and down the two of them flew on his sled, with Heidi wrapped warmly in a sack upon his knees. Outside the goatherd's hut he left her, saying gruffly, "Mind you're ready to start back before it gets too late."

The living room of Peter's home seemed miserably dark, where his mother sat sewing, and his bent old grandmother was at her spinning wheel. Heidi went to her at once, saying, "Good day, Grandmother — my Grandfather brought me down to see you, on his sled."

The two women could hardly believe it. Not of grim Alp-Uncle! Yet Heidi looked so well, and spoke so cheerfully, that they were soon forced to change their minds.

"See, Grandmother — this shutter's loose," said Heidi. "My Grandfather would soon mend that for you." Grandmother clasped her outstretched hand. "Ah, my dear child, I cannot see! Yet indeed I sometimes lie awake, fearing the hut may fall on us."

"You'd see better outside, Grandmother. Come with me, and see the white snow shine . . ."

When Grandmother explained her blindness, Heidi was miserable to think the old woman would never see the sun's warm rosy afterglow again. "My Grandfather would make you better — he can do anything —" She chattered on about all the things he made and did till she was interrupted by a noise outside, and Peter came running in, home from school.

"Peter cannot read properly," said Grandmother sadly. "I hoped he'd learn to read aloud from my old prayerbook, with its lovely hymns."

"We must soon light the lamp," murmured his mother.

Immediately Heidi sprang up to say goodbye, and ran outside. The two women exclaimed that Peter must go with her, but just then they heard Grandfather approaching, and his voice calling out, "So you're ready just at the right time!" He wrapped Heidi warmly, held her on one arm and, dragging the sled behind him with the other, began the long climb back. Grandmother went to bed murmuring, "If Heidi could come again, there would be something still to make me happy."

"Now you must mend Peter's hut tomorrow," Heidi was telling Grandfather.

"And who suggested that?" he growled.

"Nobody . . . Just me." And Heidi coaxed him so earnestly that next day he did actually mend the shutters of Peter's home, while she chattered away inside with Grandmother. However, Grandfather would only stay outside — he knew how his nearest neighbours had always thought of him.

The winter passed swiftly, with many visits to the goatherd's hut, where everything outside that clattered and banged was gradually repaired. Each evening Grandmother prayed, "If only our dear Lord keeps Heidi safe, and Alp-Uncle so good-humoured . . ."

Up on the mountain it seemed no time at all before another joyful summer had passed and another winter drew towards its close; spring would soon be there, with warm winds rustling the firs, and pasture days that Heidi thought the most beautiful on earth. Now she was nearly eight, skilled in everything her grandfather had taught her, and Little Swan and Little Bear followed her like dogs. There was nothing in the mountain life that she didn't find satisfying; she had made all its ways her own.

Then, one specially fine March day, a man dressed in sombre black climbed up the mountain: the village Pastor, once Alp-Uncle's neighbour down in Dörfli, brought a message about Heidi: "I've come to warn you that she must go to school next winter."

"Rubbish! She'll grow up here, among animals and birds. What she learns from them won't harm her. Send my grandchild every day in winter up and down the mountain?"

"Come back to the village, and live there. Make your peace with God, my friend; the villagers will soon accept you."

But Grandfather was stubborn, and the Pastor left him, muttering, "May God help you!" as he went.

A day or two later another visitor arrived — Cousin Dettie, in a smart dress and feathered hat. Her uncle looked her up and down sourly, but Dettie was unabashed: oh yes, she'd heard all about Heidi's lack of schooling! Now here was a piece of real luck — a rich man in Frankfurt had a delicate little daughter, always in a wheelchair, who needed a companion. Some unusual child, well — one like Heidi. And of course if the rich child died — Dettie broke off, meaningly.

"Take your good news elsewhere," growled her uncle.

Then Dettie stormed at him, told him everyone in Dörfli was on her side, swore if it got to court he wouldn't like the way they'd speak about him.

His eyes flamed. "Take her then, and go! I don't want to see her back with you again — nor with a feathered hat and words like yours."

He strode indoors.

"You've made Grandfather angry, I'm not coming," said Heidi, giving Dettie a terrible look at the very thought of leaving him and her beloved mountains.

"Aren't I coming back this evening?" she asked plaintively, as Dettie forced her away down the footpath. "Then can't I even say goodbye to Peter and his grandmother?"

"You don't know what a lucky girl you are," Dettie answered evasively. "You can visit Peter's grandmother later on, and bring her good white bread to eat . . ." Her grip never slackened on Heidi's hand, and so she was whisked through Dörfli and away, watched by many interested villagers, who lost no time in spreading such a fine piece of gossip. It soon reached Peter's grandmother, who lamented loudly. As for poor Heidi, she could hardly believe she'd been wrenched away with such cruel suddenness from the people and places she had grown to love more than anything in the world. When would she ever see Grandfather and Peter's grandmother again? Or hear Peter himself calling her to come with him and his herd to the high pastures, where the tangy air smelt of snow and flowers, and the eagle hovered high above them, circling in his splendid plumage on the mountain wind?

Dettie was taking her to rich Mr. Sesemann's Frankfurt home. While they stood waiting on the doorstep his twelve-year-old daughter, Clara, was in her schoolroom, eagerly expecting their arrival. "Isn't it time yet, Miss Rottenmeier?" she kept asking.

Since Clara's mother's death this woman had ruled the domestic household. Her proud expression and stiff style of dress matched one another well. She would have had things all her own way — except for Mr. Sesemann's order that nothing should be done against his Clara's wishes.

Sebastian the footman answered Dettie's ring. He handed them over to a pert parlourmaid, who led them to the schoolroom, where Miss Rottenmeier rose formally to inspect Clara's companion. Heidi was wearing her simplest dress and her tattered old straw hat. She peered up in amazement at the housekeeper's towering cap.

"What is your name, child?"

"Heidi," said Heidi clearly.

"There's no such name! What were you christened?"

"I don't remember."

"Dettie, this child is rude or simpleminded! How old is she?" Miss Rottenmeier had expected a better dressed child, with Clara's manners. She felt at once that Heidi wouldn't do.

"She was christened Adelheid," said Dettie hastily, "and she's almost ten."

"I'm just eight, Grandfather says so," put in Heidi.
Dettie pinched her.

"Eight! Then what schooling have you had?"

"None," said Heidi.

"Then how can you possibly read?"

"I can't — and nor can Peter," responded Heidi.

"Excuse me, madam, but this child's just what you asked for, when you wrote. She's unspoilt — not like some older children. Now my mistress is expecting me." Dettie curtsied and was away out of the house before Miss Rottenmeier could catch up with her to say that Heidi was unsuitable.

"Would you sooner be called Adelheid or Heidi?" Clara was inquiring.

"I'm never called anything but Heidi."

"And I've never seen a child like you before! Are you glad to be in Frankfurt?"

"No, but tomorrow I'm going home, and I'll take Peter's Grandmother some good white bread."

"You strange girl! I think we'll have fun together when you share my lessons, Heidi. They always made me yawn, before — then Miss Rottenmeier said I looked tired and gave me codliver oil!"

Heidi looked alarmed, though she was glad of Clara's friendliness. Miss Rottenmeier plainly disliked her. Sebastian was offended at table when she told him he looked like Peter the goatherd — although he smiled broadly when she put a white roll in her pocket to keep for Grandmother. In the middle of Miss Rottenmeier's lecture on table manners and how to speak to servants Heidi fell asleep. She was so tired that she was taken straight to bed.

She woke next day in a grand room, and ran to the window

to look for blue skies and firtrees, but there were only streets and houses, and the big windows were far too heavy for her to open them. To be shut in like this made her feel desperate as a caged bird, fluttering against the bars. If only there were somewhere high enough that she could climb — then surely she would see above the rooftops to her own beloved mountains? Later in the morning, when she heard the sound of fine carriages driving past with a swish of wheels, she imagined it was the rustling of her firtrees, and she rushed from the schoolroom dragging everything from the table: books, ink, and tablecloth.

"Heidi mustn't be punished, she didn't mean it," said Clara firmly.

It was Sebastian who was kind enough to open a heavy window in Heidi's bedroom for her. Together they stood and stared out at the busy city street; nowhere was a single firtree. Then Sebastian pointed to a tall church tower, not too far away, saying, "You'd get a fine wide view from up there". As soon as Heidi was alone again she ran outside to find the tower. At first she wandered unsuccessfully, until she found a hurdy-gurdy boy, with his pet tortoise, who agreed to guide her there and wait below for her, since the tower's old watchman reluctantly agreed to take her up the steep, winding stairway to the very top. But the view was another bitter disappointment for Heidi: all it showed her were more streets and houses as far as she could see.

"What does a little one know of views?" asked the tower's watchman, as he led her down again. Outside his door was a fine catbasket, loud with purring kittens. Heidi swooped on them with joy.

The old man was softened. "Would you like one?"

"For me?" She could hardly believe it: what new pleasures for Clara! Two kittens went home with her, one in either pocket,

and the hurdy-gurdy boy led the way.

"Quickly, little miss!" Sebastian greeted her. "They're at table already. Miss Rottenmeier looks like loaded cannon." he shut the door hurriedly in the hurdy-gurdy boy's face.

There was ominous silence in the room until Miss Rottenmeier began her usual scolding.

"Mew . . . mew!"

"But Heidi!" exclaimed Clara, "You can see Miss Rottenmeier's really angry — and all you say is 'mew'?"

"It's not me, it's these kittens."

"Kittens!" Miss Rottenmeier rose, and fled the room. Laughing heartily, Sebastian swore to find a safe corner where the kittens could live undisturbed. Heidi and Clara went to bed greatly pleased and comforted.

Next day the hurdy-gurdy boy rang the doorbell boldly and demanded payment for bringing Heidi home. Sebastian led him to the schoolroom, where he played specially for Clara, Heidi and their tutor. Miss Rottenmeier was even more upset to find him there, and a tortoise crawling on the floor. She didn't know how to punish Heidi.

"Wait till Papa comes home, he'll know what to make of her," said Clara soothingly. She'd grown more cheerful every day since Heidi shared her lessons. However, the little Swiss girl made no progress with her ABC, and telling Clara about her alpine life brought on most dreadful longings to go home: "I must go — I must go *tomorrow*." Clara always answered, "Wait for Papa's arrival."

The only thing that brought Heidi secret comfort was the knowledge of two more precious white rolls saved each day for Grandmother. While Clara rested she would sit alone, wondering if the pastures were still green and the little golden flowers glowing in the sun. One day she jumped up, packed some bread rolls in her big red scarf, put on her old tattered hat, and ran downstairs.

Unluckily Miss Rottenmeier was just coming indoors. "What does this mean, Adelheid? You're not to go wandering again."

"I'm not — I'm going home," said poor Heidi.

"What? Leave here, where you're spoiled with every comfort? The child's gone crazy." The angry housekeeper took her back upstairs, and when she discovered the bedroom cupboard bulging with bread rolls she grew angrier still and threw them all away.

Heidi broke into heavy sobbing. "Now Grandmother won't have any good white bread . . ." She couldn't stop crying.

Clara was just as upset by Heidi's misery. "Listen, when you do go home I'll give you lovely fresh rolls for Grandmother — truly, Heidi, just as many as you ever had."

When Mr. Sesemann returned home he went straight to Clara's room, and found both children there together. He kissed his daughter, then held out his hand, saying kindly, "And here's our little Swiss girl. Are you and my Clara friends — or do you quarrel?"

"Clara's always kind," said Heidi.

"And Heidi never quarrels," said Clara.

"Excellent —" Her father was delighted. He went to unpack the presents that he'd brought her, and was waylaid by a Miss Rottenmeier bleak with complaints.

"Adelheid's one idea is to bring dreadful people and animals into this house."

"So? But Clara seems happy and cheerful with her."

Miss Rottenmeier snorted. "Adelheid's behaviour is almost halfwitted, and she's hopeless at her lessons."

Mr. Sesemann began to feel slightly worried. He returned to Clara, and tactfully sent Heidi away to fetch a glass of water. This gave Clara a chance to explain about the hurdy-gurdy boy's tortoise, the kittens, and Heidi's impulsive way of speaking and behaving.

Her father was greatly amused. "So you don't want me to send her away?"

"Oh no, Papa. Since Heidi's been here something funny has happened every day! And she tells me about so many, many things."

Just then Heidi returned with a brimming glass of water.

"It's from the fountain," she said proudly.

"You never ran all the way to the street fountain, Heidi?" exclaimed Clara.

"Yes — and a white-haired gentleman sends his greetings to

Mr. Sesemann! He has a friendly smile and wears a thick gold chain."

"Why, that's our good old friend, the Doctor," Clara and her father cried together.

Mr. Sesemann was delighted by Heidi's original behaviour, and told Miss Rottenmeier that he found her very good for Clara, who loved her dearly. Anyway, next time he went away his own mother would be staying, and there was no one she couldn't understand or manage.

Clara was overjoyed to see old Mrs. Sesemann again, and spoke so much of 'Grandmama' that Heidi spoke of 'Grandmama' too. Miss Rottenmeier was deeply shocked, but Mrs. Sesemann herself was highly amused. "Heidi, I shall not call you Adelheid, and you shall call me Grandmama," she said. The warmhearted old lady and the homesick child pleased each other greatly. Heidi loved Grandmama's white hair under its ribboned cap, and Grandmama loved Heidi for her naturalness and serious dark eyes.

"What does this child do while Clara rests?" she inquired.

"Adelheid stays in her room, imagining silly things," replied Miss Rottenmeier.

Grandmama laughed. "I should do just the same, if I were in her place. Let her come to my room — I've brought her some illustrated books."

"Even Clara's tutor cannot teach Adelheid her ABC."

Mrs. Sesemann was surprised. "Let her come, all the same. We'll look at the pictures together."

At first Heidi was enchanted by these splendid illustrations, until she came to one showing a flock at pasture with their shepherd, all by golden evening light, when she gave a sob.

Grandmama took her hand. "Did this picture remind you of

something? Come, my child, don't cry — this book has many charming stories in it. See, now we're happy again, and you liked some of these pictures, didn't you? Once you can read you shall keep the book yourself. Now bring it with you, and we'll go to Clara.''

Soon everyone was amazed by Heidi's progress. In the evenings she read aloud to Grandmama and Clara, and was overjoyed to receive the lovely book for her very own. But since trying to run away she had grown pale, and cried more often. Of course Grandmama noticed, and asked her what was wrong, but Heidi wouldn't tell anyone, she was too afraid of sounding ungrateful.

''When one is sad and can tell nobody why'', said Grandmama very kindly, ''one takes it to the dear Lord in heaven, who helps every sorrow. Do you pray to him each evening, thank him for the good things you have, and beg him to protect you from all harm?''

''Not since I was small,'' said Heidi.

''Remember, he can help us in everything, and give us what makes us happy.''

''Can I say anything at all to him?'' Immediately Heidi ran to her own room, and poured out everything that was in her heart about her longing to be home again with Grandfather.

But nothing seemed to change. Soon Grandmama saw the sadness in Heidi's expressive eyes. ''Child, why aren't you happy, is it always the same thing?''

Heidi nodded. ''I gave up asking God. I know why he didn't hear me, so many people pray to him in Frankfurt.''

''Don't give up, Heidi! Perhaps the time's not right for you to have just what you wanted. Promise me you'll go on praying, child, don't forget God, and he'll never forget you, and will give you more than you ever asked for, in his own good time.''

Heidi gladly promised.

Everyone was sorry when Mrs. Sesemann left. Heidi read to Clara every day, but one story was so sad that she broke down entirely and wept and wept. Miss Rottenmeier threatened to take the precious book away if she ever cried like that again. So Heidi swallowed down her sobs, though there was often such a lump in her throat that she couldn't eat. She grew thin and paler still, fretting for the mountains. Autumn and winter had passed, the time was coming when Peter would take the goats to pasture among the golden flowers. Heidi's homesickness grew worse each day.

About this time an eerie feeling crept into the grand Frankfurt house, as if it might be haunted. Each morning the front door was found wide open, although there was no burglary. Sebastian spent a night on watch — but when he glimpsed a white figure on the stairs he retreated hurriedly. Next day Miss Rottenmeier wrote to Mr. Sesemann, begging him to come home. She knew how to work on him, by telling him of Clara's terror.

Mr. Sesemann returned at once, and sent round a note to his friend, the Doctor, asking him to come and watch with him one night: ''Someone tries to scare my household! We'll have weapons handy, and wine to cheer our vigil.''

At about one o'clock the Doctor whispered, ''Did you hear something — the door?''

Holding their weapons and branched candlesticks they crept outside. Moonlight was flooding through the wide open door, and on the threshold was a small figure, which turned towards them with a trembling cry. Barefoot in her white nightdress, Heidi stood staring wide-eyed at weapons and candleflame.

''Why, it's my little water-carrier!'' said the Doctor.

"My child, what does this mean?" asked Mr. Sesemann.

"Let me take her back upstairs to bed," said the Doctor kindly. He took the shivering child's hand, saying, "Be calm, and come along —". Once Heidi was tucked up in bed and had stopped trembling, he asked her, "Tell me, do you dream vividly?"

"Oh yes — each night I'm back home with Grandfather! The firtrees are rustling outside, and I run to fling the door wide open, and everything's so beautiful! But every morning when I wake I'm here in Frankfurt, and I've such a lump in my throat that I can't swallow."

"Hm. Where did you live with your grandfather?"

"High up, on the mountainside. It was so lovely there, so lovely," wept Heidi.

The Doctor laid her gently back on her pillows, saying, "Sleep now, and wake up happier. Tomorrow everything will be all right."

Downstairs he told his friend: "Your 'ghost' is merely a sleepwalker! And so homesick she's become a little skeleton. You must send her home at once."

"What!" cried Mr. Sesemann. "But she came to us so well and strong!" He was deeply upset, and at first wouldn't think of sending Heidi home till she was cured — but the good Doctor insisted, adding, "Return her to her mountain life tomorrow, or you may never send her back at all."

When she heard that Sebastian was to take Heidi home, Clara was equally upset. She tried without success to change her father's mind, and was only comforted when he promised she should visit Heidi with him later on. She began thinking of all the things that she could ask Miss Rottenmeier to pack in Heidi's trunk.

Heidi herself had just been told to put on her best dress and go to Mr. Sesemann. "What do you say to all this, child?" he greeted her. She looked at him so inquiringly that he smiled, and asked: "Has no one told you that you're going home today?"

"*Home,*" gasped Heidi. She wasn't sure if she was dreaming still, and could barely choke down her breakfast, before rushing upstairs to say goodbye to Clara.

"See what we've packed for you, Heidi!" Clara said. There were many lovely gifts — and, above all, a basket of fine white rolls of bread.

Mr. Sesemann himself led Heidi to the waiting carriage. She thanked him earnestly for everything, and begged him to thank the Doctor too. It was a long journey, and she and Sebastian spent the night in Basle, before travelling further. Heidi sat in the train clutching the precious basket of rolls, and thinking of Peter's Grandmother.

At the nearest mountain station, Sebastian made arrangements for the local baker's cart to carry Heidi and her trunk on up to Dörfli. He knew that he was meant to take her home himself, but he was scared of the rough mountain walking. Before saying goodbye he handed her a mysterious package from Mr. Sesemann, together with a letter for her Grandfather. Heidi was already shivering with excitement; when the baker lifted her down at Dörfli she pushed her way between a knot of curious villagers, saying, "Thank you — Grandfather will fetch my trunk." Then

she ran off up the path as fast as she could to Peter's hut, and went breathlessly inside.

"That's just how Heidi used to come in! Can it truly be Heidi?" exclaimed Grandmother. She stroked the child's curly head, and almost wept for joy. Very carefully, Heidi put the white rolls one by one into her lap.

"Oh, bless you, child! But the greatest blessing is to have you back," said Grandmother — while Peter's mother was busily admiring Heidi's smart new Frankfurt clothes. Heidi took off her hat and gave it to her, remembering Grandfather's last words to Dettie. Then she took off her best dress, and put on the old red scarf over her petticoat, before she said goodbye.

"Now Grandfather will know me again . . ." She went on up the Alp, her basket on her arm. The high peaks flamed with rosy evening light, the valley lay in golden mist. Every few steps she stopped to look around her, so filled with joy and delight that tears streamed down her cheeks while she thanked God that he had brought her home again.

On the bench outside his hut sat Grandfather, smoking his pipe. Before he could realise what had happened, Heidi was flinging her arms around him, crying, "Grandfather, Grandfather!" His own eyes were wet with tears as he pulled her on to his knee, saying, "So you've come home, Heidi . . . You're not looking very well."

Heidi explained all about her homesickness, and what the Doctor had said, and gave her grandfather Mr. Sesemann's letter.

"There's money in the package for you, child," he said, after reading it. "Put it away now in the cupboard, and come and have your drink of milk."

"Grandfather, there's nothing better than our milk," said

Heidi, as she drank it eagerly.

From outside came a shrill piping — it was Peter, calling to his herd.

"Hullo, Peter! Little Swan — Little Bear, do you know me still?" Heidi ran outdoors, and Peter stood staring at her in amazement; he could hardly believe she was back again. "Will you come with me tomorrow to the pastures?" he asked happily.

"Next day, perhaps. Tomorrow I must go to Grandmother."

That night she lay down contented, and slept as she had never slept in Frankfurt. Her deepest longings were all satisfied — she'd seen the mountains in the evening light, heard the whisper of the firtrees; she had come home again.

Next morning, Grandfather was to collect her trunk from Dörfli, while Heidi went to Peter's hut. As soon as Grandmother heard Heidi's step she cried out lovingly, "Is that you, child?"

"Yes, oh yes!" Heidi began to dance about the room. "Clara's father gave me some money, I can buy you good white rolls every day! You'll be cured and strong — and see again —"

Grandmother was silent, not wishing to spoil her joy. Heidi went on skipping around the room, and came across the old prayerbook. "I can read your verses now . . ." Straightway she sat down and read a hymn of thanksgiving for the sun's light after storm and stress.

"Oh child, you've made me feel so happy," said Grandmother.

As she trudged back up the mountain path with Grandfather, Heidi told him: "I can buy Grandmother lots of rolls now, but she doesn't want to take my money."

"You can buy her plenty — and still buy yourself a fine new bed, and other things."

"I like my hay bed best! You know, Grandfather, if I'd come home earlier like I prayed to, we wouldn't be so happy now, would we? We must always do as Clara's Grandmama taught me. We'll have to pray each day, and then God won't forget us either."

"Once forgotten, it's for ever," muttered Grandfather.

Heidi didn't believe it. When they reached home she fetched her precious book, and while Grandfather settled himself on the bench she read aloud her favourite story — of the spendthrift son who returned to his father's house after much wandering, and was forgiven. Grandfather was very silent. Much later, while she slept, he mounted the ladder to the loft, and stood with bowed head repeating the consoling words. At earliest dawn he stood outside to watch the light growing on the mountain and hear the morning birdsong in the firtrees.

It was Sunday. Heidi found Grandfather dressed as she'd never seen him, with silver buttons on his jacket.

"Come, Heidi, the sun's out! Put on that pretty dress, we'll go to church together." And as they went down the mountainside the bells rang out below from Dörfli.

"Just like a festival," said Heidi, enchanted.

Hardly anyone in church paid attention to the service, they were too busy whispering, "Alp-Uncle . . . Alp-Uncle's here!"

Afterwards they saw him take his grandchild by the hand, and lead her to the Pastor's house. When they emerged again the Pastor was shaking him warmly by the hand. All the people began gathering around them, as though welcoming home a dearest friend — they were remembering what Grandfather had done for Peter's grandmother. They heard him saying, "I'm going to take your advice after all, old friend, and bring Heidi back to Dörfli for the harsh mountain winters."

On a September morning in far-off Frankfurt, Clara's doctor was on his way to see her. He was a sad man now — his own little daughter had died, and he lived alone. Clara too had been ill all summer, there was no question of her visiting Heidi till next May. She was only comforted when Mr. Sesemann suggested: "Doctor! You go and visit Heidi for us!"

"I'll even take my codliver oil, Doctor, if you'll go," Clara persuaded him. "Do start tomorrow!"

Then the Doctor laughed, and promised he would set out within a few days, and take whatever presents Clara wished to send.

Miss Rottenmeier packed the things, while Clara watched: a hooded cloak, so that Heidi could visit Grandmother in all weathers; a monster of a sausage, to be divided between Peter and his family; special tobacco for Grandfather; and lastly many little packages, surprises for Heidi to enjoy. Clara could just imagine how she'd skip for pleasure. Then Sebastian bore the huge parcel to the Doctor's house.

One day Heidi woke with the dawn, to the rustling of the firtrees. Bright clouds drifted across a blue sky, and the rising sun cast a floss of gold over heights and meadows. Grandfather was already out, milking his goats. Heidi ran outside to dance a jig of sheer delight beneath the swaying branches.

Soon Peter and his herd arrived. ''Coming up with me today, surely?'' he asked, temptingly.

''No. Now I'm waiting for my Frankfurt friends.''

Peter grumbled, ''But Uncle's always here!'' and slouched away.

Heidi couldn't settle indoors, she was in and out, now dusting, now jumping around outside on the sweet-smelling grass. Suddenly she cried out: ''Grandfather — they're coming, here's the Doctor!'' And she ran bright-eyed to greet him and thank him again and again for having sent her home.

The Doctor had hardly expected her to remember him at all, and he was delighted by her warm and loving gratitude which lightened his sad heart. He was only sorry to be the bearer of bad news, and to see Heidi's face fall as he explained about Clara's illness and how neither she nor Grandmama would be coming yet.

But Heidi soon noticed his sad expression, and quickly forgot her own disappointment as she told him comfortingly: ''Spring will come quickly — and Clara will love to stay here longer. Come and meet Grandfather.''

Soon the three of them sat down together on the bench.

''You must enjoy this perfect weather while you're here,'' Grandfather was saying. ''Stay in Dörfli, and visit us daily. Now Heidi'll fetch us out our midday meal. We eat simply here, but don't you think our dining-room superb?''

''Yes — and this is where our Clara must come,'' agreed the

Doctor, as he ate and drank with appetite beneath that sparkling sky. Just then they saw one of the villagers toiling up towards them, bearing the huge surprise bundle on his back. The Doctor was first to remove the heavy wrappings. ''Now, child — unpack these treasures for yourself.''

Heidi went to and fro, from one exciting package to the next. Once she planted herself before the two old men, and declared, ''But they haven't made me happier than you have, Doctor!'' He laughed, and said he never could have believed it.

Later that day they went with him down the mountain to deliver Clara's gifts. Grandmother was specially pleased with the soft grey shawl. As for Peter, the sight of that giant sausage overwhelmed him! But by now it was getting late, and Heidi's bedtime — so off she went, holding Grandfather's hand, to their peaceful home beneath the star-studded heavens.

Next day the Doctor climbed the path early, with a furiously jealous, silent Peter and his goats. Heidi, Little Swan and Little Bear were waiting for them, all three as cheerful as the brilliant sunshine on the heights. First, Heidi led her good friend to her favourite spot. All around them shone the autumn day, on peaks, wide green valley, and crystal snowfields. The mountains raised majestic turrets high in the deep blue sky where the eagle swooped. Heidi's eyes shone.

The Doctor said quietly, ''Indeed, it's beautiful — even to a sad heart.''

''No one has a sad heart here, only in Frankfurt,'' said Heidi merrily.

''But if one brings a sad heart here, Heidi, what then?''

''Perhaps you have to wait, however sad you are, because there may be something better for you . . . only I think you have to be patient,'' she answered haltingly. His shadowed look

reminded her of the darkness Grandmother lived in, and how her favourite verses helped her. Shyly, she spoke them to the Doctor, who sat silently remembering his own childhood, and his mother reading to him.

"That's a beautiful faith you have, Heidi," he said. "Mind you hold fast to it."

Each day he wandered with her on the alp, or with her grandfather who had a special knowledge of all the herbs and flowers. At last the time came for his return to Frankfurt.

"If only I could take you home with me, Heidi! If I'm ever ill and lonely, would you visit me?"

"Oh yes — I love you almost as much as I love Grandfather!" And she waved and waved to him, just as his own daughter used to do, till he was out of sight.

The snow lay deep that Alpine winter. Peter would take his sled and slide all the way down to Dörfli, where Grandfather had taken Heidi and his goats. Once, he had shared a rambling old house there with Tobias, his only son, who had been Heidi's father; but that was long ago and since then its later owners had allowed it to fall into decay. Now Grandfather rented it, and used all his skills to make it habitable. Heidi was quite thrilled with everything — specially with one large room, where stood a huge white-and-blue-tiled stove; and on a warm ledge behind this she had her bed. There was another smaller room for Grandfather, an enormous kitchen, and a lengthy passage, strewn with straw, that could be partitioned for the goats.

Heidi went to school in Dörfli, and enjoyed it, although Peter was a constant truant — his tolerant schoolteacher thought the snow too deep for him to come. Indeed, it was so soft and deep, it prevented Heidi from visiting his grandmother, although Peter managed to visit Heidi just the same. But one day, when the

whole alp side was hard frozen and crystal-shining, he came to take Heidi up to Grandmother's. She wore the warm cloak that Clara had sent her, and chattered all the way.

Grandmother was unwell. She was lying wrapped in her grey shawl, but her face lit up when she heard them coming. "If only I'd asked Clara to send my bed from Frankfurt!" Heidi said. "Grandmother would love its big fat pillows."

"I'm lucky to have many things that some old people do without — and you to come and see me, Heidi. Will you read today? When I hear those words, child, it's as though they spread light in my heart," the old woman murmured. She lay and listened and as the children were leaving she took Heidi's hand and held it fast before she let her go.

The moon was high in the sky when Peter took Heidi home on his sled — they were like two birds flying through the air. That night she lay in her warm bed wondering how Grandmother could hear those comforting words more often; and by next day she had a plan.

"Peter, you must learn to read properly, then *you* can read to Grandmother! Do look — Clara sent me this ABC in verse, and I could help you — after school." Peter grumbled and sulked, but her coaxing won him over. Night after night they sat together at the table, Grandfather smoking peacefully beside them, smiling to himself. Outside the snow was falling heavily, and Heidi couldn't visit Grandmother again; but one evening Peter reached home saying triumphantly, "Now *I* can read! Heidi says I'm to read Grandmother verses every day."

How amazed Peter's teacher was, when he read aloud in class! What Heidi and Grandfather between them had done for him was discussed all over Dörfli — though Grandmother still yearned for spring's return and Heidi's. Peter made her much-loved verses sound quite different. He stumbled over the words, making many errors.

The house in Dörfli was abandoned when May came at last, with all its glories. Spring waters flowed down the mountain heights into the valley, everywhere were buds and flowers. Heidi was home again on the alp, running and shouting with pleasure — or she would throw herself down on the sunniest place to peer into short grass and find small insects hopping and dancing in the sun. It was as though everything on the mountain hummed and sang for joy. Then there was the familiar sound of Grandfather at work — he'd made one fine new chair, and was working on another.

"For Clara and Grandmama! And — suppose Miss Rottenmeier comes too, Grandfather? Would she ever sit on that sort of chair?"

They were interrupted by Peter's arrival, his herd pushing and shoving around him. "There!" he said, holding out a letter.

It was from Clara, at last. She wrote to say they were already packed, and she and Grandmama were looking forward to seeing them once her treatment at Ragaz was over. Miss Rottenmeier wasn't coming, alarmed by Sebastian's powerful description of Swiss ravines. "Goodbye, dearest Heidi," the letter ended, "Grandmama sends warmest greetings, your true friend, Clara."

Peter was livid to hear that more friends were coming to visit Heidi and interfere with their companionship again. He stormed away, angrily swishing his stick amongst his frightened herd.

May soon passed, and June was even more splendid with flowery scents. One morning Heidi came running from the hut with shrieks of excitement: "Grandfather, come and see, quickly!"

A train of people was winding up towards them. First two men with a carrying chair on which sat a young girl, warmly wrapped. Then came a led horse, bearing a stately lady, and behind them another man pushing a wheelchair, and yet another carrying many rugs and furs.

"It's them — it's them!" shrieked Heidi.

When the procession reached the hut, Clara and her Grandmama exclaimed with pleasure.

"My dear Uncle," said Mrs. Sesemann in her lively, friendly manner. "What a position — fit for a castle! And here's my little Heidi, blooming like a rose. Clara, child, what do you say to all this splendour?" Clara had never imagined anything like it.

Grandfather had already put rugs and furs into her wheelchair, and now lifted her into it, while all the time she was looking round her, and sighing, "If only I could run about and look at everything!" Heidi just managed to push the chair beneath the firtrees, then she ran to put a great bunch of flowers in Clara's lap. "But these are nothing to the ones on the high pastures — harebells and red centaury and some golden Sunseyes — it all smells so good and it's so beautiful you'd never want to leave it."

Meanwhile Grandfather was preparing the midday meal before the hut. Grandmama was delighted with this entrancing dining room and view — while Clara was soon ready to start on her second slice of toasted cheese. "Oh, it tastes so good —" she murmured.

"That's the mountain air," Grandfather told her. He and Grandmama were already like old friends, and it seemed to everyone no time at all until the sun was far down the sky. Already, below them, they could see Mrs. Sesemann's mount and the chairmen arriving.

"We haven't even seen upstairs inside the hut," sighed Clara.

Grandfather turned to Grandmama. "Why not leave her up here with us a while? I should look after her myself. All those rugs and furs would make her a good soft bed."

"It was my own thought too, only I scarcely liked to burden you!" exclaimed Mrs. Sesemann, smiling warmly. And soon a second hay bed, topped with a nest of rugs, stood close to Heidi's in the loft.

Farewells were said, and Grandfather accompanied Mrs. Sesemann down the mountain. She was returning to Ragaz, and would only visit them from time to time, to see how they got on.

The best experience of Clara's day came later: she lay in bed looking at the stars, and cried out, "It's like being driven through heaven in a carriage!"

"Do you know why they sparkle at us so? It's because they feel we're so happy, and so safe . . ." said Heidi drowsily. She was falling asleep, while Clara lay wakeful — for nothing so exciting as this bedroom among the stars had ever happened to her before.

Next day she watched the heights and valley appear as morning mists rolled away before the sunrays. Soon Grandfather came to help her up and carry her outside. "Oh Heidi — if I could stay here always," she said, breathing in the heady air.

"Now you see it's better than anything in the world up here with Grandfather," responded Heidi.

Their breakfast milk tasted as if sugar and cinnamon flavoured it, and Clara drained every drop. "Tomorrow two mugfuls," said Grandfather.

After midday the sun grew hotter still, and Heidi wheeled the chair under the firtrees, where they stayed chattering together, like the birdsong in the boughs above. Evening took them almost unawares. Peter passed by them in grim silence, with his goats — although Clara added her friendly, "Goodnight" to Heidi's.

"I'm so hungry here," she told Grandfather. "At home everything seemed to taste of codliver oil." That night she slept in the big soft bed as soundly as Heidi did in hers.

Grandfather became very fond of Clara. He soon began searching the high pastures for special herbs to hang in Little Swan's stall — these were to make her bloom with health so that she gave richer milk each day. When Clara had been there a little while Grandfather began helping her to stand, and every time she managed better. She and Heidi had written such reassuring letters to Mrs. Sesemann that Grandmama felt no need to make another arduous mountain journey yet.

It was the most beautiful summer on the alp. Daily the flowers opened to the sun, giving out wonderful scents, and by evening the snowfields above were drowned in a golden-flaming sea of light. Heidi told Clara frequently about the higher pastures, where the grass itself shone blue with flowers. One evening she begged Grandfather: "Won't you take us up the alp tomorrow?"

She was so jubilant when he agreed that she ran to tell Peter they might spend the whole day with him. His only response was a bearish unforgiving growl. But Heidi and Clara were thrilled. That night Clara dreamed of the high pastures starred with flowers, and Heidi of the eagle calling, "Come! Come! Come!"

Peter arrived next day to see Clara's wheelchair placed ready outside the hut. That chair — his enemy's! He looked about him, but Grandfather had gone indoors again . . . Peter rushed at the chair like a madman, and hit it so hard that it careered away, dashing downhill to disaster. So Clara would have to leave, and Heidi would come with him to the pastures every day, just as she used to do, thought Peter. He fled off up the mountain, satisfied.

"Now I'll have to go home," wailed Clara, when Grandfather discovered what had happened.

"That's odd," he muttered to himself, "the chair couldn't have got there by itself . . . Today we'll go to the pastures anyway," he told Clara cheerfully, "then we'll see." He carried her right up the mountain, Heidi following with Little Swan and Little Bear.

"I thought you were still asleep," Peter muttered, when Grandfather asked him why they'd been forgotten.

"Hm. Did you see anything of the wheelchair?"

Peter looked sullen, and Grandfather said nothing more. He settled Clara in the sunniest place, telling them he would return by evening. The children's pleasure was almost indescribable. The great snowfield above them shone with thousands of gold and silver stars. The eagle flew high above. Now and then a little goat would come and lean trustingly against Heidi, or Clara.

Soon Heidi began longing to go yet higher. First she placed bunches of grass in Clara's lap, and brought one of the goats for her to feed. Clara assured Heidi she didn't mind being left alone. It thrilled her to be responsible for feeding a little trustful, dependent animal. She put her arms around its neck, saying, "If only I could stay up here with you forever."

In a short while Heidi came running back.

"It's wonderful there today — it may never look or smell like that again! Don't you think Peter and I between us could help you walk?"

When Peter stubbornly refused to help, Heidi looked at him so darkly and so fiercely that he wondered uneasily what she knew, and gave way. Between them Clara stumbled along, supported clumsily on his right arm, her own around Heidi's neck. It was hard — but she grew steadier with each step. "Now we can go where we like," Heidi said joyfully, "and you won't need that chair again."

Clara simply sank down speechless among the flowers, while Peter curled up, slept — and dreamed of the shattered wheelchair. After a while the goats came trotting up to find them. It was long past mealtime, and Clara was helped down the alp again. There was too much food for them to eat it all, and Peter

had a double share which, together with his guilt, almost choked him.

Soon afterwards Grandfather arrived, and was delighted to hear of Clara's progress. He helped her walk a little way himself, then swung her up and carried her home, saying that by now she needed rest.

That night Heidi and Clara lay in the loft, looking out on starshine. ''You know, Clara — I prayed so much in Frankfurt to come home earlier,'' murmured Heidi, ''but if I had, you wouldn't have come here and got well, would you? Now we ought to do as your Grandmama says, and thank God for sending such happiness that you can walk . . .''

Next day Grandfather wrote to Mrs. Sesemann, inviting her to come in a week's time, although he never mentioned what new things were happening. Each morning Clara woke, feeling, 'I'm well!' With each day she grew hungrier, and drank more mugfuls of foaming milk.

When Mrs. Sesemann was due at last, Heidi and Clara sat outside the hut, waiting for her on the bench. As she rode up they stood, and walked towards her, Clara's hand just touching Heidi's shoulder. Grandmama could hardly believe it — laughing and crying together, she embraced first Clara and then Heidi; she was so happy that she couldn't speak.

Grandfather was standing by the bench, and when she reached him she took his hands in hers. ''This is all your doing, Uncle!''

''And God's sunshine and mountain air,'' he answered, smilingly.

''We must immediately telegraph my son,'' were her next words.

''Peter will take your message down to Dörfli for you.''

But Mr. Sesemann had also been planning a surprise, and was already climbing the footpath as Peter came running down. He looks like a policeman! thought Peter wildly.

"Can you direct me to 'Alp-Uncle's' hut?" called Mr. Sesemann.

Peter was quite speechless with horror — he tripped, and went head over heels, dropping his piece of paper.

"How remarkably shy," mused Mr. Sesemann, continuing his climb; while poor Peter went rolling over and over so far that he landed at the village baker's feet, to hear his mocking, "Whatever will come flying over next?"

Perhaps even he had guessed the truth about the wheelchair! Peter wanted to creep home and hide, but Grandfather himself had told him to hurry back, and 'Alp-Uncle' was someone he didn't dream of disobeying. He still lagged a long way behind Mr. Sesemann, who was soon almost at the hut — and could barely believe what he was seeing: coming towards him was a tall slender girl with blonde hair, leaning on a smaller one with sparkling dark eyes.

Clara's father thought he must be dreaming. "Is this possible? *Clara*?" He held her closely in his arms — was this truly his fragile little daughter? There was much joy and excitement all round, handshakings and huggings. Until Grandmama discovered poor Peter, who had arrived trembling all over, intent on trying to hide.

"My dear Uncle! What's the matter with this boy?"

"Ah — he's the jealous wind that rolled Clara's wheelchair away, and he's expecting punishment," Grandfather explained.

"Oh, the poor boy," exclaimed Mrs. Sesemann. "Of course he felt bitterly that Frankfurt strangers had stolen his most precious possession, his Heidi. That revenge was stupid — but

we're all stupid when upset!'' She turned to Peter. ''Come here, my lad. You did a very wrong thing — but out of it has come Clara's cure. So the wrongdoer is loser, after all, and has suffered too. Will you remember this in future, Peter?''

''Oh yes, I will,'' he replied, feelingly.

''Then we'll forget it now, and you must have something pleasant to remember us by. What shall it be?''

Peter thought of all the marvellous things he might buy in the local market. ''A tenpenny piece,'' he said.

Grandmama was laughing. ''You shall have tenpenny pieces each week for life — and I'll even put it in my will!''

Peter was overcome with relief, and could scarcely thank her. He ran off joyfully, bounding along full of happiness and excitement; he could hardly wait to tell his family.

Now the remaining company sat down to begin their delicious alpine meal. Mr. Sesemann was tactfully asking Grandfather how he could best show his gratitude, but Grandfather replied with dignity that he already shared their pleasure in Clara's cure. ''Yet I'm an old man,'' he added, ''and if you could tell me Heidi shall never have to work for strangers, that would be a rich return indeed.''

''Certainly; Heidi's like my own dear child,'' replied Mr. Sesemann. ''And our mutual friend, the Doctor, means to settle near you this very autumn; so you see, Heidi will have another good protector close at hand.''

''And what can we do for Heidi now?'' put in Grandmama. ''What would please you best, child?''

''My big warm Frankfurt bed for Grandmother, so she won't feel the cold again,'' said Heidi, all in one breath.

''You good child! It shall be here in two days,'' said Grandmama. Heidi immediately wanted to run and tell

Grandmother the news. So in the end they all went down the mountain together, Grandfather carrying Clara, and Heidi darted first into Peter's hut, crying: "Grandmother, my bed's coming from Frankfurt for you!"

It was a little while before Grandmother believed it. She truly thought that these grand Frankfurt folk were taking Heidi away from her and Peter again, but Mrs. Sesemann soon put that right. "No, Heidi stays here, and we'll come back each year to see her, where this miracle took place for our beloved Clara. As soon as we return you'll see that we've not forgotten you."

Then she and her son went down to Dörfli, while Grandfather trudged home with Clara, Heidi skipping beside them like a young chamois.

Next morning Clara was sad to think she must leave this lovely place so soon: now she was better her father wished to take her with Grandmama on a tour of Switzerland. Heidi comforted her by saying, "Next summer you'll be walking right from the start, so think what good times we shall all have together then. And you know, Grandmama is even sending us two special beds, so that you can come and stay with me in Dörfli too."

It wasn't long before Mr. Sesemann appeared, bringing Grandmama's mount to carry Clara down. Heidi and Grandfather stood waving outside the hut, till there was no longer any sign of horse and rider.

In Dörfli itself, building was quickly put in hand: the Doctor soon arrived, intent on buying the ramshackle old house where Grandfather and Heidi had been wintering. Now he decided on having it rebuilt, so that one end would be his own, and the other would have plenty of room for Heidi and Grandfather, or any of their friends. It was an arrangement that made everybody happy. He even had a snug stall built for Little Swan and Little Bear.

One day, when the two old men were talking together, the Doctor said, "My dear Uncle, you share my feelings for the child, so let me share with you in everything — I should like to look upon her as another daughter and secure her future, so you and I can leave her without care when it's our time to go at last." In reply, Grandfather only pressed the Doctor's hand, but his good friend understood the comfort that his words had brought.

At that very moment Heidi herself was with Peter and his Grandmother, who was soon begging her to read aloud her favourite song of praise and thanksgiving. When she had done, and they had all talked of the marvellous things that had been happening for them, Heidi's words came tumbling out joyfully as she imagined the happy future ahead of them, and the wonderful mountain summers she was looking forward to sharing with all her friends.